Disney
FROZEN

5-

Minute
Stories

DISNEP PRESS
Los Angeles • New York

Contents

FROZEN

The kingdom of Arendelle was a happy place. The king and queen had two young daughters, Anna and Elsa. The girls were their pride and joy. But the family had a secret. Elsa could create ice and snow out of thin air!

One night, Anna convinced Elsa to turn the ballroom into a winter wonderland. As the sisters happily played together, Elsa accidentally lost control of her magic. An icy blast hit Anna in the head, and she fell to the floor, unconscious.

The king and queen rushed the girls to the trolls, mysterious healers who knew about magic. A wise troll named Grand Pabbie saved Anna by removing her memories of Elsa's magic. He explained that she was lucky to have been hit in the head, not in the heart.

The troll told the king and queen that Elsa's powers would only grow stronger. "Fear will be her enemy," he warned.

The king and queen knew they had to protect their daughter. To keep her magic a secret, they closed the castle gates.

The king gave Elsa gloves to contain her powers, but she was still afraid she might hurt someone. She even avoided Anna to keep her safe.

Then, when Anna and Elsa were teenagers, their parents were lost at sea. The sisters had never felt more alone.

Elsa stayed inside, where she could hide her magic. But she could not keep the castle gates closed forever. On the day of her coronation, her subjects were invited inside to celebrate.

Anna was thrilled at the chance to meet new people! She had barely stepped outside when she met Prince Hans of the Southern Isles. The two instantly fell in love.

At the coronation ball, Prince Hans asked Anna to marry him. Anna said yes, and the couple went to ask Elsa for her blessing.

Elsa refused to bless the marriage. She couldn't let Anna marry a man she had just met!

Anna couldn't believe her sister. "Why do you shut me out? What are you so afraid of?" she cried.

As Elsa fought with her sister, she lost control of her magic. Ice seemed to shoot out of her hands. Now all of Arendelle knew her secret.

Panicked, Elsa fled into the mountains.

With her secret out, Elsa let her powers loose. A storm raged around her as she created an ice palace and even changed the way she looked.

Below her, ice and snow covered Arendelle. Anna felt awful! Leaving Hans in charge, she went after her sister.

As Anna trekked through the forest, she lost her horse. Luckily, she met an ice harvester named Kristoff and his reindeer, Sven. The two agreed to help her find Elsa.

High in the mountains, Anna and Kristoff came across a dazzling
winter wonderland, where they met a living snowman! "I'm Olaf,"
he said.

Anna realized that Elsa must have created him. She asked Olaf
to lead them to Elsa so she could bring back summer. Olaf loved the
idea of summer and happily led them to Elsa's palace.

Inside, Anna told Elsa about the terrible winter storm in Arendelle. "It's okay. You can just unfreeze it," she said.

But Elsa didn't know how to stop the snow. Frustrated, she cried out, "I can't!" An icy blast shot across the room and hit Anna in the heart!

Kristoff rushed to help Anna. "I think we should go," he said.

At the base of the mountain, Kristoff noticed that Anna's hair was turning white. He knew his friends the trolls could help.

Grand Pabbie saw at once that Anna was hurt. "There is ice in your heart, put there by your sister," he said. "If not removed, to solid ice you will freeze, forever."

Grand Pabbie explained that only an act of true love could thaw a frozen heart.

Anna knew Hans was her true love. Maybe a kiss from him would save her. Anna, Kristoff, Sven, and Olaf raced back to Arendelle to find him.

But Hans was not in Arendelle. He had set out to look for Anna
when her horse returned without her.

Hans and the search party arrived at Elsa's palace. The men
attacked Elsa, and she defended herself. Suddenly, one of the men
aimed a crossbow at Elsa! Hans pushed it aside, and the bolt hit a
chandelier. It crashed to the ground, knocking Elsa out.

Hans and his men took her back to Arendelle and locked her in
the dungeon.

Outside the kingdom, Anna, Kristoff, Olaf, and Sven hurried down the mountain. Anna was getting weaker by the minute. Kristoff was worried about her.

At the castle gates, he passed her to the royal servants. He was starting to realize that he cared deeply about Anna, but he knew that her true love, Hans, could make her well again.

Anna found Hans in the library. She asked him to save her life with a kiss, but he refused! Hans had only been pretending to love Anna so that he could take over Arendelle.

Putting out the room's fire, he left Anna to freeze.

In the dungeon, all Elsa could think about was getting away from
Arendelle. It was the only way to protect everyone from her powers.
Elsa became so upset that she froze the whole dungeon and escaped!

Alone in the library, Anna could only dwell on her mistakes. In trying to find love, had she doomed herself and her sister?

Just when Anna had given up all hope, Olaf arrived. The snowman lit a fire, even though Anna worried that he might melt.

"Some people are worth melting for," he said.

Olaf looked out the window and saw Kristoff returning. The snowman realized that Kristoff was the true love who could save Anna!

Olaf helped Anna outside, where she spotted Kristoff across the frozen fjord. If she could reach him in time, she would be saved!

But then she saw something else: Hans was about to strike Elsa with his sword!

Using her remaining strength, Anna threw herself in front of Elsa. Hans's sword came down just as Anna's body froze to solid ice.

Elsa wrapped her arms around her frozen sister. "Oh, Anna," she sobbed.

Then something amazing happened: Anna began to thaw!

"An act of true love will thaw a frozen heart," Olaf said. Anna's love for Elsa had saved them both.

"Love!" Elsa cried, looking at Anna. "That's it!" Elsa realized that love was the key to her magic. She reversed the winter and brought back summer.

Hans was astonished to see Anna alive. "Anna?" he said. "But she froze your heart."

"The only frozen heart around here is yours!" Anna said, and sent him reeling with one punch.

With summer restored, Arendelle returned to normal—but from then on, the castle gates were open for good. For the first time in a long while, Arendelle was a happy place again. And Queen Elsa and Princess Anna were the happiest of all, for they had found their way back to each other!

FROZEN

FAMILY MATTERS

As Olaf walked through the castle, he noticed a portrait of Queen Elsa and her sister, Princess Anna. The painting made him happy because he liked the sisters so much.

Just then, Olaf heard Elsa's voice. "Maybe the ballroom," she said.

"The ballroom's too big," Anna replied. "How about the courtyard?"

Olaf stared at the image in awe. "Wow, this painting is so realistic!" he exclaimed.

"The courtyard doesn't seem right, either," Elsa continued.

Suddenly, Olaf realized the voices weren't coming from the portrait, but from the study at the end of the hall.

"What are you doing?" he asked.

"We're planning a party," Elsa explained.

"I love parties!" Olaf exclaimed.

At that moment, Gerda and Kai entered the study.

"Good morning," Gerda said. "I've got some new flowers for you."

"And I have your hot chocolate," Kai chimed in.

Anna quickly pulled Olaf aside. "It's a surprise party," she whispered. "So you have to keep it a secret."

"I love secrets," whispered Olaf as Kai and Gerda left the room.

Elsa had an idea. "Olaf, would you like to gather supplies for the party?"

The little snowman's eyes lit up. "Really?"

Elsa handed him a list.

"Ooooh!" said Olaf. "These must be secret ingredients! You can count on me."

And before the sisters could read the list to him, Olaf raced outside and bumped right into Kristoff.

"Hi!" Olaf said. "I'm helping with the surprise party."

Kristoff grinned. "You mean the one for—"

But Olaf shushed Kristoff. "Even my list is a secret."

"Really?" asked Kristoff.

"Yes. So secret even *I* don't know what it says. See?"

Kristoff laughed. "That's because you can't read," he said. "Let me help."

Kristoff read the list to Olaf and Sven. In no time, the snowman and the reindeer were off to find the supplies!

The first item was goat cheese.

When Olaf and Sven pulled up to the Anderson family goat farm, Marte and Goren welcomed them warmly.

Goren looked at Olaf's list. "A party, eh? Our cheese wheels are a perfect party snack!"

"What are cheese wheels?" Olaf asked.

"It's how we store cheese," explained Goren. "We tried rectangles. It was a disaster."

Some of the Andersons' kids helped load the cheese onto the wagon. Olaf and Sven thanked them and headed to their next stop: the Miller family flour mill.

When the wagon halted in front of a windmill, a young girl greeted them. "Hi," she said. "I'm Nora."

"Hi! I'm Olaf, and I like warm hugs," Olaf said. Nora was happy to give him one.

"Is your windmill haunted?" Olaf asked when he saw a shadowy figure.

"That's no ghost!" Nora laughed. "That's Uncle Lasse. He's just covered in flour. Flour isn't just in our family," Nora explained, "it's in our clothes, too."

Olaf showed them his list. Uncle Lasse quickly fetched a few sacks of flour and put them in the wagon.

"Your party sounds like fun," he said. "And here's plenty of flour to bake a cake big enough to feed the entire castle!"

"I didn't know castles could eat!" Olaf said, waving goodbye.

Olaf and Sven had one last item to get: flowers from the nursery run by two sisters, Violet and Vita.

Olaf showed the sisters his list, and Violet quickly rolled up a wheelbarrow full of different flowers.

"This garden's been in our family for generations," said Violet.

"You're a family, too?" asked Olaf. "Do you have goats or ghosts?"

Vita smiled. "Families are like snowflakes—"

"They are hard to catch on your tongue!" Olaf interrupted.

"And no two are exactly alike," Vita said.

When the snowman returned to the castle, he was greeted by Anna, Elsa, and Kristoff.

"I have all the secret ingredients," said Olaf.

"Great work, Olaf!" Anna said. Then she began pulling the petals off the flowers.

Kristoff carried the flour toward the castle, and Elsa whisked away a plateful of cheese wheels. "See you at the party," she told Olaf.

"Don't forget— it's in the library!"

But when Olaf arrived at the library, he saw only Elsa, Anna, Kristoff, and Sven. "Where's everyone else?" he asked.

"This party's for our family," Elsa said. "And the guests of honor are about to arrive."

At that moment, Gerda and Kai entered. Anna and Elsa threw the colorful flower petals into the air and shouted, "Surprise!" Gerda and Kai were speechless.

"You've been family to us ever since I can remember," Elsa said with a smile. "We wanted to say thank you."

"You did all this for us?" Gerda asked.

Elsa said, "We wanted to do something nice for you."

Kai looked into his cup, which was filled with delicious frozen chocolate. "I can tell you made it!" he said.

"We added a little vinegar and salt to the flour Olaf brought us, and Anna and I used it to polish all the brass and copper in the kitchen," said Kristoff.

Olaf turned to Anna. "And you made the flowers into colorful snow?"

"Yes," Anna said. "It's called confetti."

"Hmm," said Olaf. "So what is the cheese for?"

"To eat, of course," said Kai as he took a big bite. "It's my favorite!"

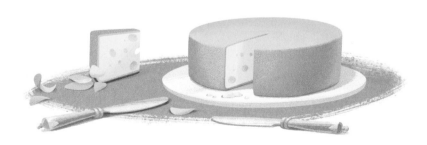

"This is a different kind of party," said Olaf.

Anna chuckled. "Well, we're a different kind of family."

"Yeah, different," said Olaf. "Just like everyone else!"

Disney Frozen

Olaf's Perfect Summer Day

Summer had finally arrived in Arendelle. Everyone in the kingdom was enjoying the long sunny days after a very cold winter.

Today was going to be the hottest day of the year so far! Most of the villagers wanted to stay inside, where it was cool.

But Olaf could hardly wait to get outside. This was the kind of day he had always dreamed about!

Olaf ran into Princess Anna's room, calling out with excitement.

"Anna! Anna! Guess what today is? It's the perfect summer day! Let's go outside and play!"

Anna groaned as she sat up in bed. "It's so hot and sticky, Olaf." But she had to smile when she saw Olaf's hopeful face.

Together, Olaf and Anna went to look for Queen Elsa. They found her in the Great Hall.

"There you are, Elsa!" Olaf cried out.

Olaf looked up shyly at the dignitary standing with Elsa. "Hi, my name is Olaf, and I like warm hugs."

"H-h-hello," the dignitary stammered in surprise. He had never seen a talking snowman before.

Olaf turned back to Elsa. "And today is the best day for warm hugs, because it's sunny. Please, can we go play in the sunshine?"

Elsa laughed. "That sounds like fun, Olaf. What did you have in mind?"

"It's so hot, though. Couldn't you cool things down just a bit, Elsa?" Anna looked hopefully at her sister.

"Olaf's always wanted to experience heat. Shouldn't we give him his special day? We'll do everything he's always wanted to do in summer!"

"You're right, Elsa," agreed Anna. "How about a picnic on the shores of the fjord?"

Olaf clasped his hands with glee. "Ooooh, I love picnics!"

Anna, Elsa, and Olaf rushed to the royal kitchen to see Olina about some picnic supplies.

"Did you bake cookies today?" Olaf asked when they got there.

Olina shook her head. "Oh, it's much too hot for baking."

"How about an ice-cold lemonade instead?" Elsa suggested.

Olaf was thrilled. "Ooooh, I love lemonade!"

Olaf, Anna, and Elsa set off for their picnic adventure.

At the royal gardens, a few children were lying on the field, too hot to play games. But Olaf didn't notice. Giggling delightedly, he ran to them.

"Hi, my name is Olaf. Don't you just love summer?" The children were charmed by Olaf, who was chasing butterflies and blowing fuzz off the dandelions.

Even Elsa and Anna couldn't resist joining in.

After a while, Anna plopped down on the grass. "Whew! I'm ready for our picnic!"

Elsa agreed. "Yes, let's head to the docks. We can sail to the shore."

Olaf, who had been chasing a bumblebee, stopped in his tracks. "I've always wanted to try sailing!"

At the docks, Anna and Elsa chose a beautiful sailboat. As they set sail, Olaf hummed happily. He even got to steer the boat!

When they reached the shore, Anna and Elsa set up the picnic. But Olaf couldn't sit still. "Don't you just love the feeling of sand on your snow?" he squealed. "Let's make sand angels together!"

The three friends spent the whole afternoon playing in the summer sun.

They built
sandcastles.

They chased
waves on the shore.

They even danced
with seagulls.

And finally, when they'd tired themselves out, Anna, Elsa, and Olaf sat down to enjoy their picnic.

"Hands down, this is the best day of my life," said Olaf.

As they sailed back to Arendelle, the setting sun made beautiful colors in the sky. Olaf was amazed. "I wish I could hug the summer sun. I bet it would feel wonderful!"

Anna smiled as she pushed her sweaty hair off her face. "You might need a bigger snow flurry for that, Olaf."

Back at the docks, Kristoff and Sven were waiting. They had spent the afternoon in icy mountain lakes. Now their sled was full of ice.

Jumping out of the boat, Anna flung herself onto the deliciously cold blocks. "Oh, am I glad to see you!"

Olaf told Kristoff and Sven all about their adventures. "I wish it could always be summer!" he said.

"Summer is wonderful," Elsa agreed,
smiling at Anna on the block of ice. "But
tomorrow, I predict a chance of snow."

LET IT GLOW

Autumn was almost gone. The chilly night air reminded Little Rock and his friends that winter was close. They had to find Grand Pabbie and get Little Rock's tracking crystal to glow before sunrise. Then he could participate in the trolls' level-one crystal ceremony.

"I'll bet there is a great clue just around the bend," said Kristoff.

Little Rock smiled. "Let's get tracking!"

Little Rock hunted for clues as the group headed up the mountain. Suddenly, he noticed a funny-looking bump under the snow. He quickly dug down deep.

"Look!" he said, popping up with an ax and a rope. "I tracked some important stuff."

"You *found* some important stuff," said Kristoff, placing the items into Sven's saddlebag. "That's not tracking. Remember?"

Little Rock nodded. He had made the same mistake before. Tracking was a difficult skill, but he needed to figure it out. Otherwise, his crystal would never glow.

"But you *did* show inventive thinking," said Anna. "And that's one of the rules of tracking, right?"

"Yes!" Little Rock answered. "Along with fearlessness and observation."

Kristoff smiled. "Would you like to hear a story about how I was inventive back when I was young?"

Little Rock nodded again. So as they began hiking, Kristoff started his story.

"When I was a kid, Sven and I were out harvesting ice one night. The northern lights were super bright, and they were reflecting on the surface of the frozen lake. Sven was going crazy trying to catch the reflections. And he finally caught one . . . with his tongue!"

Sven groaned in embarrassment while everyone else giggled.

"I tried pulling him and pushing him, but nothing worked. His tongue just stretched and stretched. I had to come up with an idea. I had to be *inventive.*

"So I grabbed a teeny-tiny ice pick." Kristoff grinned. "And I chipped away at the ice very gently, all around his tongue, until a little circle popped out. Sven pulled the ice into his mouth and it melted. Then he was free. Sven gave me a big icy-cold lick across the face, and we sat there, staring up at the colorful lights in the sky."

Little Rock laughed. "You guys have such great stories about the northern lights. I wish I had a good story to share."

As the trail curved around the mountain, everyone gasped. It ended
at the base of a giant waterfall.

There Anna spotted a mossy cloak. Everyone agreed: it was Grand
Pabbie's!

"He must have dropped it as he climbed up the cliff," said Elsa.

They gazed up, wondering how they would do the same. Sven
put his tongue in the rushing water. Then he did it again. Kristoff
understood. "He's suggesting Elsa freeze the waterfall," he explained.

"What an inventive idea, Sven!" said Little Rock.

Elsa waved her arms and the roaring water froze solid.

"Now we climb," said Kristoff.

"Be careful, Anna!" called Elsa.

"I totally got this," said Anna, striking the ice with her ax and pulling herself up. "I've always wanted to climb a waterfall!"

When Anna and Kristoff made it to the top, they threw the rope down. Elsa tied it around Sven and helped Olaf sit on Sven's head.

Once Sven and Olaf reached the top, they hoisted up Little Rock. But before they could throw the rope down again, Elsa had used her magic to build stairs!

When they asked her why she hadn't done that in the first place, she explained. "You were so excited to climb the waterfall. I didn't want to spoil anyone's fun."

From the top of the falls they followed the trail as it climbed higher and higher. Soon the air became thick with fog, and although Little Rock was nervous, he kept going.

When they reached the mountain peak, a figure appeared in the mist.

Little Rock ran over and threw his arms around it. "Grand Pabbie!" he exclaimed.

Everyone stood still, surprised.

Kristoff cleared his throat and gestured toward the real Grand Pabbie.

Little Rock was confused. He looked at the moss-covered rock he was hugging and then back at Grand Pabbie.

"I found him!" he exclaimed, running toward Grand Pabbie and giving him a giant hug. "I tracked you!"

"Hello, Little Rock," said the kindly old troll.

Little Rock anxiously pulled out his tracking crystal, and his face fell. The crystal was still dull.

"It's because I'm not very good at tracking." Little Rock sighed. Then he explained he would never have found Grand Pabbie and the other trolls without his friends. "If anyone here has earned a tracking crystal, it's all of you. Not me. I needed you, my friends, to get here."

Suddenly, Little Rock's tracking crystal started to glow!

"Look!" said Anna, pointing at the crystal.

"But I didn't earn it," said Little Rock.

Grand Pabbie nodded. "Actually, you did. You figured out what it takes to be a good tracker." For Little Rock, that meant understanding that he needed help from his friends. And that realization had made the crystal glow!

With the glowing stone in his hands, Little Rock joined the other young trolls around Grand Pabbie ready for the crystal ceremony to begin.

As Grand Pabbie lifted his arms into the air, all the trolls raised their crystals. The northern lights reflected the colors of their crystals, and the lights bounced back into the sky, slightly brighter. But not as bright as Grand Pabbie had hoped.

"Mind if I try something?" Elsa asked.

Elsa waved her arms, and her magic curled into the sky, creating a giant snowflake. It sparkled as it turned, reflecting the northern lights back into the sky and all around them!

Olaf hopped with excitement.

Elsa's and Anna's dresses shimmered, too.

"Well, now," said Grand Pabbie.

"That is so much better!"

Far away, in Troll Valley, the intense colors caught Bulda's eye.
"Everybody, look up!" she shouted. All the trolls knew what the
bright lights meant: Little Rock had succeeded in his quest!

Thanks to the level-one trolls, the northern lights were shining
strongly again, providing everyone below with magical memories.

The Ice Games

It was winter in Arendelle—the happiest winter in many years.

Princess Anna and Kristoff were inside, reading quietly in front of a roaring fire. Suddenly, the sound of children's laughter came through the open window. Anna put her book down and went to the window.

"Oh!" she said. "Come look, Kristoff. It's soooo cute!"

Kristoff joined Anna at the window. Three
children were building a sled in the snowy
courtyard below. Kristoff smiled at the children,
but Anna could see that he was thinking about
something else.

"All right," Anna said. "Out with it.
What's on your mind?"

Kristoff turned to Anna. "I didn't have a lot of friends when I was a kid," he said. "I mean, I had Sven. And the trolls. But only humans are allowed to enter the Ice Games."

"The what?" Anna asked.

"Every year on the winter solstice, ice harvesters and their families from all over the world gather on a glacier and hold the Ice Games. It's supposed to be really fun. But you have to have a three-person team." Kristoff looked a little sad. "I bet those kids are building that sled for the big race. . . ."

Anna told Elsa what Kristoff had said. "It was so sad to hear about missing the Ice Games," she said. "So I was thinking—"

"that we should take Kristoff to the games this year!" Elsa finished for her, delighted. "The three of us can be a team!"

"Yes!" Anna said, hugging her sister. "I knew you'd get it!"

Anna and Elsa quickly packed everything they would need for the journey to the games. Then they ran to tell Kristoff about their plan.

"You'd do that for me?" he asked, his face red.

"Of course!" Anna said. "Every ice harvester should get to go to the Ice Games!"

The day before the winter solstice, Anna, Elsa, and Kristoff arrived at the Ice Games. Anna couldn't help staring at the group around her. She'd never seen so many ice harvesters in one place!

"Say," one of them said, pointing at Elsa, "isn't that the queen of Arendelle? I heard she has magic ice powers."

"No fair!" said another. "She'll use her powers to win the games!"

"I promise on my honor as queen that I will not use my powers in the games," Elsa said.

"Yeah, so back off," said a gruff voice. Anna turned to see a group of ice harvesters from Arendelle standing behind her. With them were the three children she had seen outside the palace window! Anna grinned. She loved that the people of Arendelle were so loyal to her sister.

"Our queen wouldn't cheat," the little girl from Arendelle said.
"And she doesn't need to, anyhow."

It was true: Elsa didn't need to use her powers to win the first
contest. She carved a gorgeous ice statue of the rock trolls using just
a hammer and a chisel.

Next was Anna and Kristoff's event.

"I don't care what the event is. I know we're going to win!" Anna said.

"Couples ice-skating," the announcer boomed.

"Unless it's that . . ." Anna said, her heart sinking. She was a terrible ice-skater.

But Anna wasn't one to back down from a challenge. She and Kristoff gave it their all, swooping and speeding around the rink. Kristoff managed a little jump, and Anna only fell down nine times. They didn't win, but they had a lot of fun trying . . . and they did manage to come in third place.

That night, Anna, Elsa, and Kristoff had dinner with the rest of the ice harvesters. As they ate, they discussed the Ice Games.

"With Elsa's first-place finish, and Kristoff and me coming in third in ice-skating," Anna said, "we actually stand a chance of winning the Ice Games!"

"All we have to do is win the sled race tomorrow," Kristoff said.

"Good luck!" Anna heard a small voice behind her say. She turned around to see the little girl from Arendelle.

"Thank you," Anna replied with a smile. "You made the ice sculpture of the palace today, right?"

The girl nodded, blushing furiously.

"It was beautiful," Elsa said. "And I know a little something about making ice palaces!"

Grinning from ear to ear, the little girl ran back to sit with her family.

"Good luck to you, too!" Anna called after her.

"What a sweet little girl," Elsa said. "She reminds me of someone else at her age."

"Me?" Anna asked.

"I said 'sweet,' Anna. Not 'annoying,'" Elsa replied with a wink.

Anna punched her sister playfully.

"Of course I meant you, Anna," Elsa admitted.

"One more round of hot chocolate?" Kristoff suggested.

"Yes, please!" Anna and Elsa said together.

As the sun rose the next morning, Anna, Elsa, and Kristoff piled into their sled. It was time for the last event.

"Here we gooooooo!" Anna shrieked. The trio rocketed down the slope with the rest of the racers.

Anna squinted against the wind as their sled went faster and faster. Soon they had pulled ahead of the other racers.

"We're winning!" she yelled.

Anna, Elsa, and Kristoff were almost to the finish line when a sled passed them. It was moving so fast they could barely make out who was inside.

It was the children from Arendelle, streaking down the slope and crossing the finish line!

"We won! We won!" the kids yelled, hugging each other and jumping up and down. Watching them celebrate, Anna couldn't bring herself to be disappointed that she, Kristoff, and Elsa hadn't won.

She just hoped Kristoff wasn't too upset.

"I'm sorry we didn't come in first, Kristoff," Elsa said later, as they took their place on the winners' podium.

Kristoff grinned. "Nah," he said. "Don't be. I finally got to compete in the Ice Games! And I think it's great that they won. Having friends you can count on is really important when you're a kid."

Anna hugged Kristoff. "Having friends you can count on is really important forever. And I have the best friends of all!"

Little Brothers!

"I am so excited to see the little snowmen!" Olaf exclaimed. "I can't wait to welcome them to the family!" He made his way up the stairs to the ice palace, high on the North Mountain. "First I'm going to hug little Sludge and then little Slush and little Slide and little . . ."

Olaf threw open the doors to the palace. Dozens of snowgies scampered around the huge icy room.

"Hi, little guys!" Olaf shouted. "Wow, you're really having fun up here!"

But the snowgies didn't stop to greet Olaf.

"Hey, Marshmallow! Isn't it exciting that we have little brothers?" Olaf called out to the giant snowman.

Marshmallow sighed. He looked tired.

Olaf turned toward one of the snowgies who was running by.

"Nice warm hug for you, little—*oof!*" The snowman careened off Olaf and landed on Marshmallow.

"Aw, look at these little guys. They're so cute!" Olaf said. "Am I right?"

Marshmallow lifted a snowgie off his shoulder and sighed again.

"Um, Marshmallow?" Olaf said. "I know you love playing with our little brothers, but would it be okay if I took a turn?"

"Come on, guys, let's play!" Olaf continued.

As he tried to gather some of the snowgies into a group, he slipped and landed on his back. "Whoa! The floor's all slippery. Slippery? Hey, that means . . . we can *skate*! I just love skating!"

Olaf got to his feet and twirled around. "Follow me, little brothers!"

Marshmallow shook his head and went outside.
"Huh," Olaf said. "I guess Marshmallow
doesn't feel like playing right now.

"How about we give warm hugs?" Olaf asked. He tried to hug each snowgie. But not one of them stopped to return Olaf's hug. They all scampered away.

"Oh," Olaf said. "So you want to keep playing? That's fine. Just stay inside so nobody gets lost."

Unfortunately, the snowgies were already headed out the door.

"Well, outside is good, too. And Marshmallow is out there. Maybe he wants to play now," Olaf said, following the snowgies.

Marshmallow seemed to be playing a new game that Olaf had never seen, which included sticking icicles into the ground. He used the icicles to form a playpen around the snowgies to keep them contained.

Olaf wanted his little brothers to use the icicles to slide down the mountain with him.

Instead, they were forming a line going up the stairs, and Marshmallow was at the head of the line!

"Hey! What's everybody doing?" Olaf asked. He had never seen the snowgies looking quite so orderly and behaved.

Marshmallow lifted the first little snowman onto the top of the banister. Then he gave the snowgie a firm push.

The snowgie slid down, down, down the banister! *Swoosh!*

"Hey, that looks fun!" Olaf said.

One by one—and then two by two—the snowgies took their banister rides.

"This is a great idea, Marshmallow," Olaf said.

No matter how quickly Marshmallow sent the snowgies down, the line was not getting any shorter. The snowgies raced back up the stairs because they wanted to slide down the banister again and again.

The sliding continued until dark, when the snowgies finally seemed tired out. They shuffled back inside the ice palace, where they piled up on top of each other.

Before long, almost every snowman was snoring, even Marshmallow.
Olaf was the only one still awake. He looked at the snoozing
snowmen and smiled. "My little brothers are the best brothers ever!"

TROLL TREK

Princess Anna was reading a story to the village children. "'That night, the young trolls climbed the highest mountain and grabbed stars out of the sky. They tossed the stars to each other and bounced them off the moon. The dancing lights woke the humans. They gazed at the stars, admiring the display and wondering what was causing it. Suddenly, the lights stopped and everything was still again.'"

Anna sat down to finish the story. "'Back in the Land of Trolls,
the troll parents demanded their children put the stars back. And the
little trolls obeyed . . . sort of.'"

Delighted, the children clapped their hands.

"Are trolls really real?" a girl named Mari asked.

Anna smiled. "They're not quite like the trolls in the story, but they're real," she said. "Just ask Kristoff."

"How do you know?" a boy asked Kristoff.

Kristoff told them he'd been raised in Troll Valley. All the children gasped.

"Where's Troll Valley?" Mari asked.

"I can't tell you," said Kristoff. "It's a secret."

The children groaned in disappointment as they collected their things and prepared to leave. But Mari lingered behind.

"Do you mind if I ask you a few questions?" she said to Kristoff. "Did you grow up by a stream? What types of flowers did you smell during spring? Is it true trolls sleep all day?" Mari wrote down everything he said.

Anna told Mari where she could find troll books in the royal library. Mari wanted to know everything about trolls. But most of all, she wanted to find out for herself if trolls were real.

After hours inside the royal library, Mari headed home with an armful of books.

She stayed up late, reading and trying to separate fact from fiction. When she found an ancient map that mentioned trolls, she studied it and used her notes from her talk with Kristoff to create a map of her own.

The next day, Mari woke up bright and early. She finished her
chores as fast as she could, and without saying a word, she grabbed
her things and left. Before long, her parents noticed she was gone.

Worried, thinking she was lost, Mari's parents rushed to the castle. Anna and Elsa gathered others to help search for Mari.

The villagers looked around the kingdom while Anna, Kristoff, and Elsa hurried into the mountains. They were certain Mari had gone in search of the trolls.

Kristoff suggested they talk to Grand Pabbie. "He'll know what to do."
When they arrived in Troll Valley, Kristoff approached a large boulder
that unrolled, revealing Grand Pabbie. "Have you seen a little girl
wandering around?"

"I have not," said Grand Pabbie. "But Little Rock and I will help you
find her."

"You cover the east side of Troll Valley, and Little Rock and I will cover the west," Grand Pabbie said to Kristoff, Anna, and Elsa. "Then we'll meet back here."

And with that, the group split up in search of Mari.

Meanwhile, Mari was walking up the mountain. She stopped beside a knotty oak tree. When she heard the gentle sound of water, she traced her finger across her map. Kristoff had mentioned a stream. "Aha!" she said.

She followed the water for quite a while before seeing the same knotty tree. "Oh, no," she said. "I just made a circle." She looked up at the setting sun and began to wonder if searching for trolls had been a good idea.

Mari sat down to examine the map more closely.

As Little Rock and Grand Pabbie crested the hill, they spotted her and stayed out of sight. They had an idea as Mari started off again. They would secretly help her find the way.

With their help, Mari was on track to reach Troll Valley! The trolls rolled themselves up into boulders, creating the edge of a pathway for Mari.

Soon Anna, Kristoff, and Elsa found her.

"Mari!" Anna called to her. "I'm so glad we found you. Everyone has been so worried."

Mari hung her head. "I'm sorry," she said. "I just wanted to find the trolls." Mari looked at Kristoff. "So . . . is this where you were raised?"

Suddenly, Kristoff's adoptive mother, Bulda, popped open and blurted out, "Of course it is! He lost his first tooth right over here."

"You *are* real!" Mari gasped. She gave Bulda a hug. When the
trolls came out of hiding, Mari realized they had helped her find Troll
Valley. "All of you were with me!"

They nodded and smiled. Mari greeted each one and vowed to
remember all their names.

That night, after Anna, Elsa, and Kristoff had led Mari back to her grateful parents, Mari decided to create a troll story of her own. Visions of all the wonderful things she could include filled her head as she drifted off to sleep.

Olaf Waits for Spring

One chilly morning, Olaf found his friends preparing to travel up into the mountains.

"Hi, Kristoff! Hi, Sven!" Olaf said. "Where are you going?"

"It's almost spring, so I have to check on my ice-harvesting equipment," Kristoff replied.

"Spring?" Olaf said. "What about summer?"

"Well, spring comes before summer. And spring has amazing things, too. We can go sailing! Just wait and see!"

"I love summer, so I must love spring—I think," Olaf said as he headed inside the castle.

Elsa was in the dining hall talking to Olina. "In the spring we'll have fresh fruit, and with fruit we can make pie," said Olina.

"Ooh, I love pie!" Olaf said. "Wait, what's pie?"

Olina smiled. "It's a delicious dessert. Just wait and see."

Olaf raced outside to find Anna.

"Spring is arriving soon!" he cried. "With sailing and pie!"

"Ah, I love spring," she said. "That's when all the cute little baby animals are born. Just wait and see!"

Olaf was excited. "I'm going to find the best place to wait for spring," he told himself. And off he went!

Olaf walked and walked, looking for a place with a good view. He wanted to see all the boats and pies and baby animals when they arrived. He had to just wait and see.

So he tried waiting in one place . . . and then another . . . and then another even better place. And there Olaf waited.

Eventually, Olaf's friends came looking for him.

"Olaf!" Anna exclaimed. "Where have you been? You've been gone for hours."

"I was just waiting," Olaf said.

"Waiting for what?" asked Anna.

"For spring, of course!" he replied. "I'm so excited that it's almost here!"

"Because as soon as it arrives, we'll go sailing . . .

and enjoy fresh pies . . .

and best of all, greet the spring babies!"

"Olaf," Elsa said, "spring doesn't arrive all at once. It's gradual."

"Sailing can be difficult at the beginning of spring," Kristoff said, "because there's still ice in the fjord. It might be a while before it's warm enough for us to go sailing in a smaller boat."

"And it doesn't get warm overnight," Anna said as they walked toward the town.

"Look in the tree," Elsa said. "The birds are preparing for their spring babies."

"Do you see the nest, Olaf?" Anna asked. "First comes the nest, then the eggs. After that, the baby birds will hatch."

"If we keep going this way," Kristoff said, "we might just find a warm, sunny spot where—"

"Ooh!" Olaf gasped as they went up a hill. "Spring!"

The next day, with Elsa's help, they even managed to go on a spring boat ride.

"This is only the first day of spring. It will get warmer soon," Anna said as she and Kristoff huddled under some blankets. "It just takes time."

"That's okay," Olaf said. "I even love *waiting* for spring!"

As it turned out, Olaf didn't need to wait very long. In just a few weeks, spring was appearing everywhere.

"Ohhh," he sighed. "Summer is great, but you know what? I love spring, too!"

ACROSS THE SEA

Anna and Elsa were going on a trip to visit some neighboring kingdoms. As they climbed aboard their ship, the captain scurried over.

"Your Majesty," he said to Elsa, "I don't think we'll make it to our first stop on time. Not with waters this still."

"Don't worry," Anna said, taking the wheel.

"We've got it covered," Elsa said, creating a light snow flurry to push them along.

Soon the ship arrived at its first port: the kingdom of Zaria.

"Welcome, Queen Elsa and Princess Anna!" King Stebor called in a booming voice.

"We cannot wait to show you our kingdom," Queen Renalia added.

First the king and queen of Zaria invited the sisters to lunch, where Anna and Elsa enjoyed tasty new foods. Then the queen took Anna and Elsa on a tour of her prized gardens. The sisters had never seen so many amazing flowers!

That night, the girls were treated to a grand festival.

"We've heard so much about your special talents," Queen Renalia said to Elsa. "Won't you show us some of your magic?"

Suddenly, Elsa felt very shy. She nodded at the dance floor.

"Would you like to join the dancing, Your Majesties?" she asked, changing the subject. "That looks like fun."

The next stop on Anna and Elsa's tour was a kingdom called Chatho. The sisters met Chatho's ruler, Queen Colisa, in front of her impressive palace.

"Thank you for having us, Your Majesty," Elsa said.

"Of course," the queen responded. "I am very happy you are both here!"

Queen Colisa first took the sisters on a walk through the kingdom's rain forest, where they saw many unique animals.

Anna was particularly fond of some bashful furry creatures.

"Why, hello there!" she said, waving at the animals.

After their walk, the queen led Anna and Elsa into an enormous gallery. Chatho was known for its striking art and relics.

As Anna admired Chatho's treasures, Elsa spoke with the queen. "These are beautiful," she said.

"I'm so glad you think so," Queen Colisa replied. "Would you like to add a sculpture to our collection?"

Suddenly, Elsa noticed a block of ice under a spotlight, ready to be carved. Once again, she felt a wave of shyness.

Noticing her sister's discomfort, Anna jumped in. "Um . . . sure! Ice sculptures are actually my specialty!"

Later, as they got off their ship in the next kingdom, Anna asked Elsa why she didn't want to show off her powers.

"I guess I just got nervous," Elsa admitted.

Anna was about to reply when she spotted someone surprising: the Duke of Weselton!

"What are *you* doing here?" Anna asked. The sisters had purposefully avoided Weselton on their tour. Their final stop was the kingdom of Vakretta, far from the Duke's home.

The Duke smoothed his coat. "I am visiting my mother's cousin's wife's nephew, if you must know. Although I wish I weren't. If I were you, I would turn my ship around right now."

The sisters looked at each other.

The Duke sighed. "Vakretta is having the hottest summer in years. Of course, you wouldn't care about *that*."

As the sisters followed the Duke into the village, they noticed Vakrettans sprawled out, sweaty and tired.

"Whoa," Anna remarked.

For once, Elsa didn't feel shy. She knew she had to do something to cool the people down. She quickly conjured some snow clouds, much to the delight of the villagers.

"It's working!" the Duke cried in surprise.

Elsa started making frosted mugs out of ice. "Why don't you get us some lemonade?" she asked.

Soon Vakretta was a frozen wonderland.
The citizens ice-skated and built beautiful snow castles.

"I suppose a thank-you is in order," the Duke said. "I frankly
don't know where to begin. . . ."

"Well, you could grab a board," Elsa suggested, winking at Anna.

The Duke turned red and started sputtering. "A duke would never . . .
it isn't . . ."

"It's okay. We'll show you how it's done," Anna called as she and Elsa
grabbed some planks and slid down a hill.

A few hours later, it was time for Anna and
Elsa to return to Arendelle. They waved to their new
friends from the ship.

"Did you have a good trip?" Anna asked her sister.

"I did," Elsa replied as she created an icy blast of snow
to direct them homeward. "I'd say it was the best
royal tour ever . . . until next time, that is!"

The Ghost of Arendelle

One afternoon, Anna and Olaf were in the royal library when Olaf spied a large pink book.

"Ooh! I like this one!" Olaf said. "Wait. What's it about?"

Anna read the title aloud: "'How to Find a Ghost.'"

"I love ghosts!" Olaf announced. "What's a ghost?"

"Well, it's . . ." Anna smiled and put her book down. "I have an idea. Follow me!"

Minutes later, Anna and Olaf burst into Elsa's office.

"Elsa!" Anna said. "Olaf wants to learn about ghosts, and I think—"

"We should have an indoor campout and go looking for one!" Elsa finished.

"Exactly!" Anna said.

Hours later, Elsa gathered some snacks from the kitchen, and
Anna grabbed lots of pillows and blankets from their bedrooms.
Then they met Olaf and began to look for a dark, spooky room they
could use.

They ended up in an old, unused portion of the castle.

"I can't wait to learn about ghosts!" Olaf said.

"Let's make a fire and roast marshmallows first," Anna said.

"Ooh, I just love warm fireplaces!" Olaf declared.

After the sisters had eaten their fill of roasted marshmallows and Olaf had created a sticky marshmallow tower, they settled down with their blankets and pillows.

"Is it time to learn about ghosts?" Olaf asked.

"Yes," Anna said. "You go first, Elsa!"

Elsa laid the book on her lap and began to read. "'Long ago, on a dark night in Arendelle . . .'" she whispered. She continued her story as Olaf listened, wide-eyed.

A while later, Elsa heard Anna snort. Anna had fallen asleep.

"Well, Olaf, I guess my ghost story made Anna pretty tired. Come
to think of it, I'm tired, too!" Elsa said as she yawned and snuggled
down under her blanket. "Maybe we'll find a ghost tomorrow."

"I'd like to meet a ghost," Olaf said before blowing
out the candles.

Soon both sisters were sound asleep.

But Olaf couldn't rest. He wanted to meet a ghost as soon as possible! As he looked through the book, he remembered something Elsa had read to him. Apparently, ghosts got lonely and wandered around at night.

"Sometimes I get lonely and wander around at night, too!" Olaf said. "Maybe the ghost and I could wander together!"

As Olaf walked down the hallway, he noticed how dark it was. The only light came from the windows! He looked right, and he looked left. He looked up and down. But he didn't see any ghosts.

"Hello?" Olaf said aloud. "Ghost? I'm here to be your friend!"

But nobody answered.

Olaf turned a dark corner at the end of a hallway, and then—

THUNK!

THUMP!

THUMP-THUMP-THUMP.

THUMP.

Olaf tumbled down

a staircase!

THUMP!

Anna and Elsa woke with a start.

"What was that?" they asked in unison. Then, "I don't know!"

"And where is Olaf?" Anna asked.

Elsa lit some candles, and they wandered into the hallway.

"Oooh!" came a little voice from the bottom of the staircase.

Anna gasped. "That sounded like—"

"A ghost?" Elsa said.

They crept down, down, down the stairs.

"Hello? Are you there, Sir Ghost?" Elsa said.

"We want to be your friends!" Anna added.

"Oh-oh-oh! I want to be friends, too!" the ghost said.

Anna and Elsa stopped short.

"Are you ghosts?" the ghost said.

"Wait," said Anna suspiciously.

Elsa quickly pulled off the sheet.

"Oh! I can see again!" Olaf exclaimed. "Thank you, ghost that looks just like Elsa!"

"I *am* Elsa!" she replied with a laugh.

"Oh, okay," said Olaf. Then he pointed to Anna. "And you are . . . ?"

"Anna," said Anna.

"Olaf, you made this our best ghost hunt ever!" said Anna.

"But I didn't find any ghosts," Olaf replied.

"Well, maybe you didn't, but you became the best ghostlike snowman we've ever seen!" Elsa declared.

Snow-and-Tell

It had been a few months since Olaf had helped Anna and Elsa end the eternal winter in Arendelle.

And as one of the kingdom's newest residents, he wasted no time in exploring his home.

Olaf loved seeing new sights, hearing new sounds, and smelling new smells.

One day, Olaf happened upon a group of children. "A parade!" he squealed. "I love parades."

"Hi, Olaf," a girl named Lisbet said. "What are you doing today?"

"Just wondering around town," Olaf replied.

"You mean 'wandering,'" she said.

"No. Wondering . . . I'm wondering, why are you parading inside when it's so nice out?"

"It's not a parade." Lisbet giggled. "It's school." Then she followed her classmates into the building.

Olaf was curious. He'd never been to a place called school before.

Peering through the window, Olaf saw Lisbet. She was in front of the class, sharing her collection of seashells. They were different shapes, sizes, and colors. "My shells are special to me because my papa is a fisherman. He sails a boat to many different places. And he always brings shells back to me from his trips."

Then the teacher, Ms. Halvorson, welcomed Olaf inside. "Would you care to join us?" she asked.

"Really? Could I?" Olaf asked.

"We're having show-and-tell," said Lisbet.

"Ooooh," gasped Olaf. "I love show-and-tell! That's my favorite. What is it?"

Ms. Halvorson explained that the students were sharing their collections: groups of items that had special meaning for them.

It was Finn's turn next.
He poured smooth, shiny
marbles into his hand
for the class to see.

Olaf noticed that
collections could be
made up of all sorts
of things, like marbles,
rocks, figurines, or
even fish!

Olaf loved hearing about all the different collections the children had brought in. Suddenly, he raised his hand. "Ms. Halvorson, can I share my collection, too?" Olaf asked.

"I think you mean, '*May* I share my collection,'" Ms. Halvorson said.

"Of course!" Olaf said.

She smiled. "Go ahead, Olaf. It's your turn."

"Hi, I'm Olaf," he said, "and I like warm hugs! I collect them from everyone I meet."

Ms. Halvorson smiled again. "Olaf, collections are usually made of things you can touch."

Olaf's eyes lit up, and he nodded with excitement.

First Olaf pulled off his carrot nose.

Then he reached
up and took a handful
of snow from his flurry.

Next he pulled out
an icicle with the tip
broken off from
behind his back.

It was certainly an unusual
collection! He placed each item on
Ms. Halvorson's desk.

"Olaf," Ms. Halvorson began, "I don't think you understand. Items in a collection have value or meaning."

"Yes."

"They're unique."

"Right."

"They're special in some way."

"Gotcha."

Ms. Halvorson looked at all the items on her desk. "Usually we collect things that aren't just parts of our bodies."

But Olaf pointed out that his carrot nose was not just part of his body. It was the first gift he'd ever received.

"This carrot reminds me of the day I met my friends Anna and Sven," Olaf explained. "When Anna gave me the carrot to use as my nose, Sven was so cute! He kept trying to kiss it! So whenever I see it, it makes me smile."

One of the children raised her hand. "What's special about snow?"

Olaf pointed to the small cloud over his head. "This is my own personal flurry. My friend Elsa gave this to me," he said. "She said snowmen didn't last long in the summer sun. Now, wherever I go, I think of her friendship."

Ms. Halvorson began to understand. "And the icicle?"
Olaf held it to his eye.

"I used this to watch for my friend Kristoff when he returned to the castle to save Anna," he explained. "It reminds me what true love looks like."

When Olaf had finished sharing, he looked at Ms. Halvorson.

"Ms. Halvorson, your eye's melting," he said.

With a smile, Ms. Halvorson wiped away a small tear.

Then the entire class cheered as they came up to hug the little snowman. Olaf was thrilled. His collection of hugs had just grown a lot.

FROZEN II

One evening, Anna and Elsa's father, King Agnarr, told them a story about the Northuldra, people from an enchanted forest. They had lived in peace with the people of Arendelle, but then everything changed, and the two sides went to war. Angered spirits trapped both groups in the forest, but King Agnarr—then only a child—managed to escape.

After the story, Queen Iduna soothed the girls with a lullaby about Ahtohallan, a special river that was said to hold all the answers to the past.

Many years had passed, and though their parents were gone, the girls had found family in their best friends, Kristoff, Sven, and Olaf.

They spent countless evenings together hanging out, having dinner, and playing games.

One night, during charades, Anna struggled to guess what Elsa was acting out. She could tell something was bothering her sister.

"Are you okay?" Anna asked.

"Just tired," said Elsa, forcing a smile. "Good night," she added as she abruptly left and went upstairs.

Moments later, Anna appeared at Elsa's door. "You're wearing Mother's scarf," she said. "You do that when something's wrong."

Though Elsa refused to admit it, something *was* wrong. Someone—or something—was calling to her.

Later that night, Elsa found herself answering the mysterious voice. As she began using her icy powers, she could feel them changing. They grew stronger and stronger until finally, she triggered a shock wave that flew across the kingdom. Fire vanished from the torches; the fountains and waterfalls dried up; even the wind died down. Villagers stumbled over the rippling cobblestones, and everyone headed for stable ground.

Once everybody was safe on the cliffs above Arendelle, the ground rumbled once again. Boulders rolled in and popped open, revealing trolls. Grand Pabbie quickly approached the girls. He explained that Elsa had woken the spirits of the Enchanted Forest.

Grand Pabbie told Elsa to follow the voice north. Then he quietly told Anna that she should go along to protect her sister. "I won't leave her side," said Anna.

The sisters, along with Kristoff, Olaf, and Sven, traveled north in search of the forest. But when they found the forest entrance, a wall of mist surrounded it. It wouldn't let Kristoff and Olaf pass through.

But Elsa felt a tug toward the mist. She took Anna's hand and stepped forward, and the mist sparkled and pulled back, providing a path for the whole group.

Once they were inside the forest, the Wind Spirit, Gale, appeared. It picked them up and whipped them around. Elsa used her magic to protect Anna from a flying branch, and Gale took notice. The Wind Spirit forced the others out, holding Elsa in her vortex.

Finally, Elsa sent out a blast of magic to free herself, and beautiful ice sculptures appeared. Each one captured a different moment in time. Elsa had never created anything like them before!

Olaf reminded his friends of his theory that ice could reveal the past. "Water has memory," he said.

Soon the trapped
Northuldra and
Arendellians from
Anna and Elsa's old
bedtime story appeared.
Anna recognized one
of the soldiers. It was
Lieutenant Mattias, their
father's official guard.

The Northuldra noticed that the sisters' scarf was Northuldra.
Whoever had saved the king from the forest must have been a
Northuldra! The Arendellians and the Northuldra believed Elsa's
magic was the key to their freedom.

The two sides argued about who was responsible for their entrapment in the forest, until a bright flash of fire appeared. The Fire Spirit dashed around the trees, setting them ablaze. Elsa used her magic to chase it down and discovered the spirit was a small salamander. The voice called, and Elsa and the salamander both turned toward it.

"You hear it, too?" she asked the salamander. The salamander scurried up a rock, and Elsa realized she needed to keep going north.

Later that evening, one of the Northuldra explained the symbols on the scarf to Elsa. They represented the four spirits. The Northuldra woman pointed out a fifth spirit, which was called the bridge. Some said they had heard it call out the day the forest fell.

Elsa was now certain that she had to follow the call she had been hearing in order to set everyone free.

Anna and Olaf joined Elsa, and the three continued north. When they reached the top of a hill, they gasped at the sight below. It was their parents' ship. They realized this must mean that their parents had been in search of Ahtohallan when they disappeared. They were searching for answers about Elsa's powers.

Elsa vowed to find the mysterious river, even if it meant crossing the dangerous Dark Sea.

Despite Anna's protesting, Elsa had to go alone. She waved her hands, creating a boat, and sent Anna and Olaf sliding in it down a path of ice. "Elsa, what are you doing? No, no!" cried Anna.

They couldn't stop, and soon they found themselves gliding down a river. Anna noticed Earth Giants sleeping on the shore. Using a branch, Anna directed their boat away from the Earth Giants and over a waterfall.

When Elsa reached the Dark Sea, she stood on the shore. Ferocious waves rose and crashed before her.

She sprinted out onto the water, creating frozen snowflakes at her feet. But the strength of the waves quickly knocked her down. Elsa clawed her way to the surface and climbed up on a giant rock. She took a breath and dove in.

The Water Nokk, an enormous horse, emerged and began tossing her around.

Elsa created an ice bridle and swung onto its back. At first it bucked, trying to throw her off, but before long the two were rhythmically riding through the mountainous waves to the far shore.

Once safe on the sand, Elsa looked the majestic creature in the eye and bowed. The Water Nokk lowered its head respectfully. Elsa smiled as it shook its mane and disappeared back into the sea.

Meanwhile, the waterfall had carried Anna and Olaf into a cavern. A strong gust of wind brought in a swirl of Elsa's magic. It was a signal that she had safely crossed the Dark Sea! The magic formed an ice sculpture before them, revealing a memory of the past.

Now Anna knew why the spirits had evacuated Arendelle, and how to free the forest. Armed with renewed strength and wisdom, she was ready to set things right.

Elsa trudged through terrible winds and thick snow. When she finally reached Ahtohallan, the mysterious voice quieted. Suddenly, just as the words of her mother's lullaby had promised, everything became crystal clear. Elsa knew she had followed the right path and was where she was meant to be.

The journey had changed both her and her sister. And together, they could restore peace and mend a broken land.